Scion®

SANCTUARY

D1552152

Publisher's Cataloging in Publication Data
(Prepared by The Donohue Group, Inc.)

  Scion. Volume four : sanctuary / Writer: Ron Marz ; Penciler: Jim Cheung ;
Inker: Don Hillsman ; Colorist: Justin Ponsor.

    p. : ill. ; cm.

  Spine title: Scion. 4 : sanctuary

  ISBN: 1-931484-50-3

1. Fantasy fiction. 2. Adventure fiction. 3. Graphic novels. I. Marz, Ron. II. Cheung,
Jim. III. Hillsman, Don. IV. Ponsor, Justin. V. Title: Sanctuary VI. Title: Scion. 4 : sanctuary.

PN6728 .S35 2002
813.54 [Fic]

Scion®

SANCTUARY

Ron **MARZ**
WRITER

Jim **CHEUNG**
PENCILER

Don **HILLSMAN II**
INKER

Justin **PONSOR**
COLORIST

Troy **PETERI**
LETTERER

CHAPTER 22

Karl **MOLINE** · PENCILER
John **DELL** · INKER
Matt **MILLA** · COLORIST

CHAPTER 26

Jason **KEITH** · COLORIST

CHAPTER 27

Lee **MODER** · PENCILER
Roland **PARIS** · INKER
Jason **KEITH** · COLORIST

CrossGeneration Comics **Oldsmar, Florida**

SANCTUARY

features Chapters 22 - 27
of the ongoing series
SCION

On the techno-medieval world of Avalon, a tale of two princes is told. What started with a mysterious sigil ended in war. Prince Ethan of the West-ruling Heron Dynasty was graced with a mark granting him power, resulting in the accidental scarring of Prince Bron of the East-ruling Raven Dynasty during ritual combat.

War between the enemy kingdoms was declared. When the battle was met, first victory belonged to the Herons, but Ethan's oldest brother and heir to the throne, Artor, was brutally slain by Bron. Ethan swore vengeance, and set out for Raven lands.

Not long after, Bron was imbued with power by Mai Shen, who revealed herself to him as a member of the godlike First. Bron then murdered his father, framed his sister Ashleigh for the crime, and took the throne for himself.

Ethan confronted Bron in the Raven Keep but was defeated, managing to escape with his life thanks to Ashleigh's help. The Raven princess was, in fact,

in Scion

Ethan

Ashleigh

Skink

Exeter

Nadia

part of the Underground movement dedicated to freeing the genetically engineered Lesser Races.

After witnessing the aftermath of a Raven-led slaughter of Lesser Races and an encounter at an illegal genetic facility, Ethan promised his loyalty to the Underground. The news came as a shock to his brother Kai and sister Ylena, who were leading a Heron invasion force at the request of their father, King Dane. Intending to find a new home for the Lesser Races, Ethan and Ashleigh voyaged to the undersea city of Haven, leaving behind their companions Skink, the former bounty hunter Exeter and the mysterious traveler Nadia. Disappointed when their pleas for sanctuary were refused, Ethan and Ashleigh finally gave in to their mutual attraction while still in Haven.

Meanwhile, Kai and Ylena led their invasion force into a narrow pass, unaware the Raven army waited in ambush.

ETHAN IS THE YOUNGEST PRINCE OF THE HERON DYNASTY.

THE HERONS AND THE RIVAL RAVEN DYNASTY HAVE BEEN ENEMIES FOR AS LONG AS EITHER CAN REMEMBER, THEIR MUTUAL HATRED BOILING OVER INTO A WAR THAT LASTED CENTURIES. FINALLY A TENUOUS PEACE WAS STRUCK, AND OPEN WARFARE WAS REPLACED BY AN ANNUAL TOURNAMENT OF INDIVIDUAL COMBAT.

BUT AT THE MOST RECENT TOURNAMENT, ETHAN VIOLATED THE RULES BY PERMANENTLY SCARRING PRINCE BRON OF THE EAST. THE ACT WASN'T INTENTIONAL. ETHAN'S ARM HAD BEEN MARKED WITH THE SYMBOL YOU SAW, AND HE WAS UNABLE TO CONTROL THE POWER IT GAVE HIM. BUT THE DAMAGE HAD BEEN DONE.

WAR AGAIN FLARED BETWEEN THE HERONS AND THE RAVENS. I KNOW ETHAN STILL FEELS PERSONALLY RESPONSIBLE FOR IT, EVEN THOUGH WHAT TRANSPIRED WAS BEYOND HIS CONTROL. HE HELPED BRING ABOUT VICTORY AT THE FIRST BATTLE...

...BUT COULDN'T PREVENT THE DEATH OF HIS ELDEST BROTHER, *ARTOR,* AT BRON'S HANDS.

ETHAN VOWED HE'D EXACT VENGEANCE FROM BRON AND JOURNEYED BACK TO RAVEN LANDS.

BUT BY THAT TIME BRON HAD SECRETLY *SLAIN* HIS FATHER AND TAKEN THE OBSIDIAN THRONE FOR HIMSELF.

EVEN MORE, BRON *ALSO* HAD BEEN GRANTED A MEASURE OF POWER SIMILAR TO ETHAN'S.

ETHAN WASN'T PREPARED FOR BRON'S NEWFOUND MIGHT WHEN HE CONFRONTED HIM. HE BARELY ESCAPED WITH HIS LIFE, AND ONLY *THEN* WITH ASHLEIGH'S HELP.

SHE'S BRON'S SISTER, IF YOU HADN'T REALIZED ALREADY, BUT *BLOOD* IS PROBABLY THE ONLY TRAIT THEY SHARE.

ASHLEIGH'S CHIEF CONCERN IS THE LESSER RACES. SHE'S PART OF THE UNDERGROUND, WHICH IS INTENT UPON OBTAINING *FREEDOM* FOR THE LESSER RACES.

NOW ETHAN HAS PLEDGED HIS LOYALTY TO THE UNDERGROUND AS WELL, DESPITE THE PULL HE FEELS FOR HIS FAMILY'S PLIGHT.

THAT'S WHAT HE AND ASHLEIGH ARE TRYING TO DO NOW, FIN A NEW *SANCTUARY* FOR THE UNDERGROUND...

...SOMEWHERE THE LESSER RACES CA BE FREE AND SAFE.

AND WHAT ABOUT *YOU,* SKINK?

YOU TALK ABOUT ETHAN, BU YOU NEVER SAY MUCH ABOUT YOURSELF.

THERE'S NOT MUCH TO SAY, NADIA.

I JUST TRY TO LOOK OUT FOR HIM.

AND *HIM?*

EXETER?

HE WAS A BOUNTY HUNTER, THE MOST FEARED IN RAVEN OR HERON LANDS. HE'D NEVER FAILED TO BRING IN A MARK...

...UNTIL ETHAN *DEFEATED* HIM AND SHOWED HIM MERCY. EXETER'S SINCE HAD A CHANGE OF HEART AND TAKEN UP THE UNDERGROUND'S CAUSE.

AN INTERESTING CHOICE TO RECRUIT SUPPORT FOR THE UNDERGROUND.

I IMAGINE ETHAN THINKS IF OTHERS SEE *EXETER* BELIEVING IN FREEDOM, THEY MIGHT ALLOW *THEMSELVES* TO BELIEVE IN IT AS WELL.

SKINK, THE UNDERGROUND WANTS FREEDOM FOR THE LESSER RACES, YET *YOU'RE* STILL ETHAN'S SERVANT.

WHY IS THAT?

ETHAN TREATS ME AS AN *EQUAL.* HE ALWAYS HAS.

I SERVE HIM OUT OF THE OBLIGATION OF *FRIENDSHIP,* NOT *SERVITUDE.*

WHICH IS WHY WE WAIT HERE FOR HIS RETURN.

THERE'S BEEN LITTLE TIME TO GET ACQUAINTED SINCE YOU JOINED US, NADIA. YOU'VE SHARED ALMOST *NOTHING* OF YOURSELF.

YOU'VE ONLY SAID YOU WERE A *TRAVELER.* WHERE DO YOU HAIL FROM?

FAR AWAY.

I WANTED TO SEE WHAT *ELSE* AVALON OFFERED.

NOW I FIND MYSELF IN A LAND TORN BY *WAR.*

THE INVASION CONTINUES EVEN AS WE SIT HERE. ETHAN'S BROTHER AND SISTER LEAD THEIR TROOPS TOWARD THE RAVEN CAPITAL.

THE COMING BATTLE MAY WELL DECIDE THIS WAR'S OUTCOME...

THERE...

...THEY'VE RETURNED.

YOU SEE, SKINK? YOUR CONCERN WAS UNNECESSARY.

ETHAN'S *FINE*.

I KNEW HE *WOULD* BE.

NEWS?

A BATTLEFIELD TRANSMISSION HAS BEEN RECEIVED FROM THE EXPEDITIONARY FORCE, SIRE.

A GREAT DEAL OF THE MESSAGE WAS *GARBLED,* BUT WE'VE RECONSTRUCTED AS MUCH OF IT AS WE COULD.

IT'S...*NOT GOOD.*

DANE?

THE RAVENS WERE WAITING IN AMBUSH WHEN THE EXPEDITIONARY FORCE PASSED THROUGH THE FELGARD NOTCH.

IT WAS A *MASSACRE.*

THOSE FEW WHO WEREN'T *BUTCHERED* FLED ALONE OR IN SMALL GROUPS.

MARIELLA, THERE'S *NO SIGN* OF KAI OR YLENA.

OUR CAPTORS NEVER SHARED NEWS OF THE WAR, MY PRINCE.

DOES THE CONFLICT *FAVOR* US?

I'M NOT REALLY SURE.

NOT *SURE*, MY PRINCE? WELL, AT LEAST THE *TOURNAMENT ISLE* IS OURS, AND THE RAVENS NOW *OUR* PRISONERS.

NO. I'M AFRAID *YOU'LL* HAVE TO LEAVE THE ISLAND AS WELL.

I'M... NOT SURE WE UNDERSTAND, SIRE.

IT'S OUR *DUTY* TO SERVE OUR KINGDOM'S CAUSE. WE HAVE NO WISH TO BE *RELIEVED*.

YOU *DO* MISUNDERSTAND. YOU'RE NOT *BEING* RELIEVED.

I'VE COME TO THE TOURNAMENT ISLE FOR REASONS HAVING NOTHING TO DO WITH THE *WAR*.

I'VE COME TO CLAIM THE ISLAND AS A *SANCTUARY* FOR THE UNDERGROUND...

...SO THE LESSER RACES HAVE A PLACE THEY CAN BE *FREE*.

...YOU SHOULD BE PLEASED. YOU WERE ABLE TO TAKE THE ISLAND WITHOUT THE LOSS OF A SINGLE LIFE.

WE ACCOMPLISHED *THAT MUCH*, AT LEAST.

THOUGH FRANKLY WE'LL NEED TO ACCOMPLISH *MORE* THAN RUNNING OFF A HANDFUL OF GUARDS FROM A DESOLATE ISLAND.

ANY VICTORY IS WORTH ENJOYING, ETHAN.

I WANTED TO ASK YOU SOMETHING *ELSE*.

YOU AND ASHLEIGH SEEM MUCH *CLOSER* THAN YOU DID BEFORE YOUR JOURNEY TO HAVEN.

DID SOMETHING *HAPPEN* BETWEEN THE TWO OF YOU?

I GUESS YOU'VE KNOWN ME TOO LON[G] FOR ME TO HAVE MUCH CHANCE OF HIDING SOMETHING FROM YOU, SKIN[.]

YES, WE'RE *TOGETHER* NOW. I WAS FINALLY ABL[E] TO ADMIT HOW MUCH I CARE ABOUT HER.

THAT'S GOOD.

I'M GLAD *YOU* THINK SO. I DOUBT YOU'D HEAR MUCH AGREEMENT FROM MY PARENTS.

OR MY BROTHER AND SISTER.

THOUGH I DON'T SUPPOSE I SHOULD REALLY BE WORRYING ABOUT *THEIR* REACTION.

THEY'RE ALREADY GOING TO DISOWN ME FOR BEING A *TURNCOAT*.

I CAN'T MAKE IT MUCH *WORSE* BY BEING WITH THE ENEMY'S SISTER.

I THINK THERE ARE MORE *IMMEDIATE* THINGS YOU SHOULD BE CONCERNED ABOUT.

LIKE HOW WE'RE GOING TO *HOLD* THIS ISLAND WHEN THE KINGDOMS FIND OUT WHAT WE'VE DONE?

BELIEVE ME, THAT *HAS* CROSSED MY MIND.

BEFORE, I ONLY HAD TO CONTEND WITH THE RAVENS BEING AN OBSTACLE. NOW MY *OWN* KINGDOM COULD BECOME ONE.

WE'VE PUT OURSELVES SQUARELY BETWEEN THEM, SKINK.

LITERALLY.

BUT I DO BELIEVE THIS PLAN HAS A CHANCE OF SUCCEEDING.

IF EVERYTHING HAPPENS THE WAY IT'S SUPPOSED TO. AND IF I CAN *RELY* ON THIS POWER I HAVE.

I REALIZE WE'VE DONE THE *EASY* PART BY TAKING THE ISLAND.

KEEPING IT IS GOING TO BE THE REAL TEST.

HAVE FAITH, ETHAN. GOOD *DOES* TRIUMPH.

I'LL GO SEE WHAT KIND OF FOOD STORES ARE LEFT AND PREPARE SOMETHING.

REST.

BOLD COURSE OF ACTION, TAKING A WHOLE *ISLAND* FOR YOURSELF.

NOT FOR MYSELF. FOR THE LESSER RACES. FOR A SANCTUARY.

THERE'S NO NEED TO SOUND APOLOGETIC. I'VE ALREADY SAID THE CAUSE YOU'RE PURSUING IS A NOBLE ONE.

SLAVERY OF *ANY* KIND IS DEPLORABLE.

NADIA, YOU'VE STAYED WITH US SINCE WE MET...

...EVEN THROUGH SOMETHING *DANGEROUS* LIKE THIS.

YOU'VE STAYED WITH US, AS FAR AS I CAN TELL, WITHOUT MUCH *REASON*.

WE HAVEN'T EVEN HAD A CHANCE TO *TALK*.

SO... ...TALK.

ALL RIGHT.

I KNOW SKINK'S TOLD YOU WHO I REALLY AM. WHO MY *FAMILY* IS, I MEAN.

IMAGINE MY SURPRISE TO FIND I'D HAD MY LIFE SAVED BY AN ACTUAL *PRINCE*.

WHAT ABOUT *YOU?* ALL YOU'VE BEEN WILLING TO SAY IS THAT YOU'RE A TRAVELER.

YOU WON'T EVEN SAY WHERE YOU'RE FROM, THOUGH IT'S OBVIOUS YOU'RE NOT FROM EITHER THE RAVEN OR HERON LANDS.

WHO *ARE* YOU, NADIA?

WELL, I HOPE YOU WON'T BE DISAPPOINTED TO LEARN I'M *NOT* A PRINCESS.

I'VE BEEN CIRCUMSPECT BECAUSE I *AM* VERY MUCH A STRANGER IN A STRANGE LAND.

BUT I OWE YOU *HONESTY* AT THE VERY LEAST.

I SAID I WAS FROM FAR AWAY. I MEANT IT.

I'M FROM *TIGRIS,* TRULY THE OTHER SIDE OF THE WORLD FROM HERE.

WE'VE ISOLATED OURSELVES FOR SO LONG, I CAN UNDERSTAND WHY MOST PEOPLE DON'T EVEN BELIEVE MY KINGDOM IS *REAL.*

OUR ANCESTORS WERE *AGAINST* THE FORCED LABOR OF THE LESSER RACES, SO THEY ABANDONED BOTH THE RAVEN AND HERON KINGDOMS.

THEY SET OUT ACROSS THE OCEANS AND FOUNDED THEIR OWN KINGDOM. THEY LABORED FOR THEMSELVES...

...AND EVENTUALLY BUILT *MACHINES* THAT LABORED FOR THEM.

AT LEAST NOW I UNDERSTAND WHY YOU WERE SYMPATHETIC TO THE UNDERGROUND'S CAUSE.

WHY DID YOU *LEAVE* TIGRIS?

RIGHT NOW I'M HELPING *YOU.*

GOOD.

I HAVE A FEELING WE'RE GOING TO NEED IT.

HE LED US STRAIGHT INTO THE TEETH OF THAT AMBUSH, THEN *LEFT US* TO OUR FATE.

RECRIMINATIONS ARE USELESS NOW, BROTHER.

WE NEED TO CONCENTRATE ON GETTING HOME.

...TURNED INTO A *MASSACRE* AT FELGARD NOTCH. HEARD MAYBE A FEW DOZEN ESCAPED...

...AND *THEM* SCATTERED ALL OVER THE COUNTRYSIDE. RIGHT RETRIBUTION FOR THE ROUT AT POINT KORDAY.

KING BRON'S PROVEN HIMSELF, AS FAR AS *I'M* CONCERNED. HE'S NOT SQUEAMISH ABOUT *WIPING OUT* THE HERONS...

...UNLIKE HIS *FATHER.*

HOLD.

MAYBE A LITTLE *TOO* ANXIOUS TO WIPE THEM OUT. I'M ALL FOR TAKING THE FIGHT TO *THEM*...

...BUT PUTTING THE WARSHIPS TO SEA AND LEAVING OUR COASTLINE UNPROTECTED, I DON'T KNOW...

YOU HEARD?

I DID.

LET'S GET DOWN TO THE WATERFRONT AND SEE IF WE CAN FIND OUT WHEN—

ANCESTORS.

THE HERONS WILL NEVER EXPECT THIS.

WE'LL BE SACKING THEIR CAPITAL BEFORE THEY EV REALIZE WE'RE THERE

Oh, YES...

ETHAN!

THEY'RE COMING!

WHAT?

WHO'S COMING, NADIA?

THE RAVEN FLEET. I WENT FOR A WALK THIS MORNING, DOWN TO THE DOCKS, AND I SAW THE SHIPS.

STILL FIVE OR SIX LEAGUES OUT TO SEA, BUT DEFINITELY HEADING FOR THE HARBOR.

YOU CAN *SEE* THAT FAR?

I CAN.

THEY MUST BE COMING TO THE ISLAND TO LAY ON SUPPLIES.

THEY CAN'T *POSSIBLY* KNOW WE'RE HERE.

THEY WON'T FIND THEIR GARRISON WHEN THEY COME ASHORE.

WE'LL HAVE TO BE *WELL CONCEALED* IF WE'RE TO HAVE ANY HOPE OF THEM MOVING ON.

IT'S *HIM*...

...AND AT LEAST ONE OF THE RAVEN SOLDIERS WE SENT OFF THE ISLAND.

THE FLEET MUST HAVE PICKED THEM UP.

WHICH MEANS THEY *DO* KNOW WE'RE HERE.

IT WOULD HAVE BEEN BETTER IF THOSE SOLDIERS HAD NEVER LEFT THE ISLAND...IF YOU TAKE MY *MEANING*, ETHAN.

THAT WASN'T A NECESSARY OPTION AT THE TIME, EXETER.

LET'S WORRY ABOUT WHAT WE'RE *GOING* TO DO, INSTEAD OF WHAT WE *COULD'VE* DONE.

IT LOOKS TO BE NEARLY THE ENTIRE FLEET.

BRON MUST BE READYING A WESTERN *INVASION*. THAT'S THE ONLY EXPLANATION THAT MAKES SENSE.

IF HE HAS ENOUGH MIGHT TO INVADE YOUR HOMELAND, WE STAND NO CHANCE OF *HOLDING* THIS ISLAND.

I DOUBT IT'S THE *ISLAND* HE'S INTERESTED IN...

...AS MUCH AS IT IS *ME AND ASHLEIGH*.

SHE'S DUE BACK *SOON*, ETHAN.

NOT SOON ENOUGH, SKINK.

AND EVEN WHEN SHE DOES RETURN, DO YOU REALLY THINK IT WILL BE ENOUGH TO HOLD THE ISLAND?

NOT *NEARLY*.

WE'RE LEFT WITH ONE CHOICE. IF IT'S *ME* BRON WANTS, THAT'S WHAT WE'LL GIVE HIM.

THE REST OF YOU CAN CONCEAL YOURSELVES. MAYBE ONCE IT'S SETTLED BETWEEN ME AND BRON...

...*ONE WAY* OR THE OTHER...

...THE FLEET WILL LEAVE.

NO. *THAT'S* NOT A NECESSARY OPTION EITHER.

WE'RE CLOSE TO ACCOMPLISHING THE IMPOSSIBLE. TO MAKING A DREAM *REALITY*.

AND SOME DREAMS ARE WORTH *FIGHTING* FOR.

YOU TAUGHT ME THAT, ETHAN.

THE THREE OF YOU GO PREPARE A SECOND LINE OF DEFENSE, HIGHER UP, NEAR THE ARENA.

WE'LL MAKE THEM *EARN* EVERY BIT OF THIS ISLAND.

EXETER, YOU CAN'T DO THIS *ALONE*. YOU'LL BE—

THIS IS WHAT I AM *BEST* AT, ETHAN.

WHEN THE RAVENS LAND...

...THEY'LL FIND *ME*.

STEP LIVELY, YOU LOT...

...FAN OUT THROUGH THE STREETS.

SEARCH EVERY BUILDING, EVERY ALLEY. *FIND* THE KING'S SISTER AND THE HERON PRINCE.

KILL ANYONE ELSE YOU COME ACROSS, BUT *THOSE TWO* MUST BE TAKEN ALIVE, OR YOU'LL ANSWER TO KING BRON HIMSELF.

HE'LL BE ASHORE PRESENTLY, AND FOR *ALL* OUR SAKES, WE'D BETTER HAVE WHAT HE WANTS.

WHAT ARE WE *DOING* HERE? WE SHOULD BE SPILLING HERON BLOOD, NOT RUNNING THE KING'S ERRANDS.

THAT'S THE SORT OF TALK THAT'LL GET YOUR *OWN* BLOOD SPILLED, BOY.

KEEP YOUR MOUTH *SHUT,* AND YOU'LL KEEP YOUR *HEAD* ON YOUR SHOULDERS.

SPOOKY, THIS, SEEING THE TOURNAMENT ISLE DESERTED LIKE—

GAAGH!

THIS ISLAND HAS BEEN CLAIMED BY THE UNDERGROUND AS A *SANCTUARY* FOR ALL LESSER RACES...

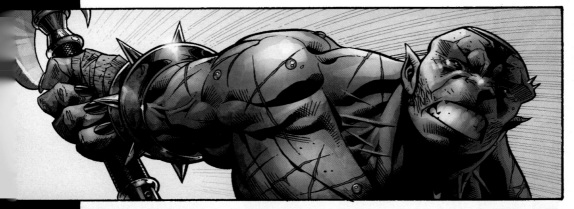

"I SHOULD BE STANDING AND FIGHTING *WITH* EXETER..."

...NOT LEAVING HIM ON HIS *OWN* LIKE THIS.

ETHAN, YOU *KNOW* THIS IS THE ONLY HOPE WE HAVE OF HOLDING THE RAVENS...

...OF *HOLDING OUT* UNTIL ASHLEIGH RETURNS.

BY LETTING EXETER *SACRIFICE* HIMSELF? THAT'S A HIGH PRICE TO PAY FOR—

BWOOM

WHAT WAS *THAT?*

THUNDER?

NO, IT CAME FROM THE *HARBOR.* IT SOUNDED LIKE...

...CANNON FIRE.

FIRE!

HOW DID THEY *FIND* US?!

THERE'S NO REASON THE HERON FLEET WOULD EVEN BE AT *SEA!*

THIS HAD TO BE A *TRAP,* WITH *ETHAN* AS BAIT. WE'LL BE BOTTLED UP AND BLOWN TO—

CHOOM

SPOOSH

I AM A PRINCE OF THE HERON DYNASTY, YET I CAME HERE TO CLAIM THE TOURNAMENT ISLE AS A *SANCTUARY* FOR THE LESSER RACES.

BUT YOUR *WAR* FOLLOWED ME HERE.

LEFT TO YOUR OWN DEVICES, YOU RAVENS AND HERONS WOULD DESTROY *EACH OTHER* AND *ANYONE* CAUGHT IN BETWEEN.

I TRIED TO VIEW THE CONFLICT AS SOMETHING *SEPARATE,* SOMETHING I COULD TURN MY BACK UPON.

I WAS *NAÏVE* TO THINK SUCH A THING. BUT UNDERSTANDING THAT I CAN'T *IGNORE* THE WAR DOESN'T MEAN I HAVE TO *ACCEPT* IT.

I WAS RESPONSIBLE FOR *STARTING* THIS WAR...

...AND *I* WILL BE THE ONE TO END IT!

HOW COULD *HE* COMMAND ENOUGH POWER FOR THAT DISPLAY?

ENOUGH POWER TO *DRIVE* THE FLEETS FROM ONE ANOTHER.

WE MUST... →KOFF KOFF←

...*STOP* THIS CONFLICT...

...OR HE'LL *DESTROY* US.

HOW, DANE?

HOW DID ETHAN *DO* THAT?

I KNEW MY SON HAD BEEN TOUCHED BY GREATNESS...

...BUT I *NEVER* REALIZED HE WAS CAPABLE OF SUCH A THING.

ETHAN?

WHAT...

...WHAT *HAPPENED* TO HIM?

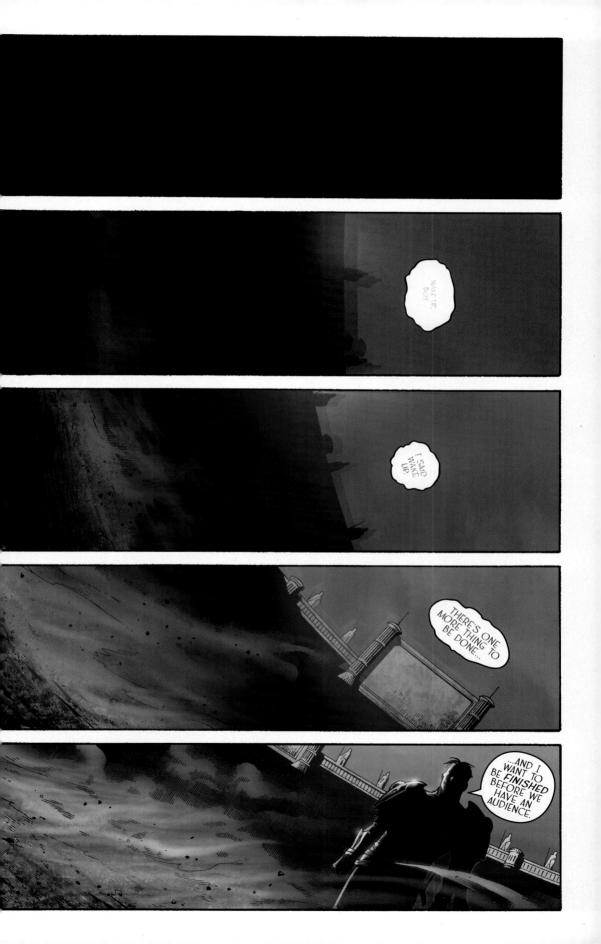

THIS IS KING DANE.

ETHAN'S FATHER.

SIRE, THIS IS ASHLEIGH, PRINCESS OF THE RAVEN DYNASTY. SHE AND ETHAN ARE...

...FRIENDS.

I'M PLEASED TO FINALLY MAKE YOUR ACQUAINTANCE.

I'M HONORED.

I'M TOLD YOU AND ETHAN HAVE CLAIMED THE TOURNAMENT ISLE AS A SANCTUARY FOR THE LESSER RACES.

MY SON IS HEADSTRONG, BUT HE'S NOT A FOOL. WHAT ARE YOU PLAYING AT, RAVEN-SPAWN?

NOTHING. THERE'S NO TREACHERY HERE, IF THAT'S WHAT YOU MEAN. ETHAN MADE THESE DECISIONS WITHOUT MY INFLUENCE.

I WOULD HEAR THAT FROM HIS LIPS, NOT YOURS. WHERE IS HE NOW?

I WISH I KNEW.

YOU BEAT ME *ONCE*...

...BUT ONLY BECAUSE YOU WERE GRANTED *POWER*.

I'VE BEEN GIVEN THE *SAME* GIFT...

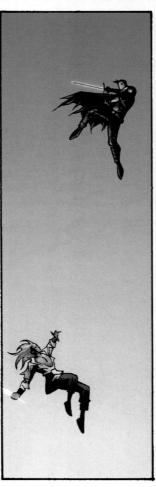

...AND YOU WON'T STAND AGAINST ME!

I'VE SEARCHED THE SHORELINE AROUND THE HARBOR AND BEYOND.

NO SIGN OF ETHAN.

I HAVE BURIED *ONE* SON, AND LIKELY HAVE LOST TWO *OTHER* CHILDREN.

I WILL NOT ACCEPT THAT ETHAN IS *GONE*...

...PARTICULARLY WHEN A *WITCH* OF RAVEN BLOOD IS TO BLAME.

ASHLEIGH IS NOT TO BLAME. SHE HAS BEEN ETHAN'S *SAVIOR*, AS WELL AS HIS LOVER.

HOW *DARE* YOU!

WHO ARE *YOU* TO SPEAK TO ME SO?!

I AM A FREE MAN IN A FREE LAND.

I HATE TO *DISAGREE* WITH YOU IN PUBLIC, FATHER...

WHAT'S THE MATTER, WHELP?

WHAT IS IT YOU *EXPECT*, BRON?

YOU WANT *ME* DEAD...

I WILL SAY *THIS*— YOU'RE FINALLY GOING TO PAY THE *PRICE* FOR WHAT YOU DID TO MY BROTHER.

FOR WHAT YOU DID TO YOUR OWN *FATHER*.

THEN COME *COLLECT* IT.

NNG!

ETHAN *IS* HERE...

...AND SO IS *BRON*!

BUT... HOW CAN BRON EVEN BE *ALIVE*?

WE HAVE TO GET *DOWN THERE!* WE HAVE TO *HELP* ETHAN!

NO.

NO? SKINK, WHAT ARE YOU TALKING ABOUT? ETHAN *NEEDS* US!

THIS TEST HAS BEEN A LONG TIME IN COMING FOR ETHAN.

HE MUST FIGHT THIS BATTLE ALONE.

NNGF!

UFF!

WELL, THIS...

~KOFF KOFF~

...THIS ISN'T QUITE...WHAT I'D PLANNED...

Hn.

YOU AND ASHLEIGH DESERVE EACH OTHER, YOU KNOW.

I CAN'T DECIDE WHICH OF YOU I HATE MORE.

I KNEW ASHLEIGH WOULD KILL ME GIVEN THE CHANCE. YOU...

...I DIDN'T THINK YOU HAD THE COURAGE.

YOU WERE WRONG.

All you have in this world, all you can truly depend upon, is your own two hands. My entire life has taught me that.

My name is Elijah. I am a slave. Or at least I was born one, and have known nothing else in my life. I am of the Lesser Races, and in Raven lands, slavery is the only lot the Lesser Races have ever been permitted.

But now another possibility exists. It is a dream we dared not ponder, a word we dared not whisper.

Freedom.

I grabbed my chance at it with both hands. I had toiled in the master's fields since I was old enough to walk, as did my mother and father before me. They're gone now, my father to his reward in the next life, my mother sold to another master when she became too aged to work in the fields.

There on the borderlands we were untouched by much of what transpired in the capital to the west. Bron's ascension to the throne did not change our lives in any way. The war itself between the Ravens and the Herons meant little to us.

But what was born of that war meant everything – an island of Sanctuary, a place of true freedom that would welcome my kind as free men. Or so said the rumors that spread even to my remote region.

So there were those who decided the lure of freedom was worth risking the punishments reserved for escaped slaves. Chyrizah and Kayanan, myself and Borzhoy the Elder, four of us...

...and only four. The rest of the estate slaves chose to remain shackled to the lives they knew, no matter how abhorrent, rather than have the courage to seek a new life. Who am I to judge their choices?

Our absence was discovered quickly, more quickly than even we had expected. Perhaps we had been revealed by one of our fellows seeking to curry favor with the master. It would not have been the first time such a thing had occurred.

The master was not an unusually cruel man, nor was he overly kind.

He was simply a human.

We fled through the fields separately, believing our chances would be better if we could split the attention of our pursuers.

We shared a common goal, a malfunctioning section of the far fence that let out onto the deeper forest. Stalks of wheat, a crop that had been my duty to tend and harvest, whipped at my arms and face, stinging reminders of the servitude I was so desperate to leave behind.

I fled with the master's shouts and the baying of his hounds in my ears, feeling as though my feet scarcely touched the ground beneath them.

I have never run so fast.

Borzhoy the Elder was not fast enough.

He was an old man, and well past his prime. In thinking on it now, with the clear perspective of hindsight, I wonder whether escape truly had ever been his intention. I think, perhaps, he'd always meant to give the master and his overseers an easy target to pursue, allowing the rest of us to slip away into the night. He bought us our chance at freedom with his life.

I can never repay the debt. I will never forget it.

We had arranged to meet under a great tree on the shores of the swamp to the north. Again, it was Borzhoy who had suggested the swamp, once having been there himself as part of a work party. He believed the treacherous terrain would discourage any pursuers who still might have dogged our trail, and so it was.

Chyrizah and I had grown up together, while Kayanan had been bought and brought to the estate. To be thrust into such a wild place was far beyond any of our experiences.

I had never in my life ventured beyond the estate's
perimeter. Until I stepped through that fence and
into the night beyond, the entirety of my world had
consisted of the fields and the slave quarters, and upon
occasion as a child, a venture inside the main house.

The unfamiliarity of our surroundings bred unease in us,
the muffled and somehow secret sounds of the swamp only
adding to it. Even the ground beneath our feet seemed
insubstantial, as if threatening to draw us in and swallow us.
But our fear was outweighed by the intoxication of being
free, truly free, for the very first time.

A meager fire had never shed so much warmth, food scavenged from such a rotted place had never tasted so sweet, and the fellowship of others had never been so rich.

You live in a narrow world as a slave. You understand all the harms that could befall you, and you make your peace with them. You accept that state of fear because there is no other choice, and because there is a certain security to so intimately knowing the threats facing you.

We had traded the dangers we knew for a host we did not. We began to believe we could survive in this new world.

But the world has teeth.

A single night had not even passed, and we'd lost two of our number. I felt despair's cold hand around my heart and heard its voice in my head. It told me those who had stayed behind, those whose fear outweighed their courage, had been the wiser, that we were fools soon to die for daring to hope.

I comforted Chyrizah as best I could through that long night, realizing that in all the world, we had only each other.

We pressed on. If Chyrizah harbored doubts she did not express them, and I kept my fears to myself.

We pushed north, intending to be gone from Raven lands as quickly as possible before turning west toward the sea. The land began to open to us.

I scarcely could have believed the whole of the world was so vast. The vistas before us, bathed in sunlight, showed me the world's true face was one of magnificence, not the drab countenance I had known since birth.

I never could have imagined sights so beautiful, and yet I beheld them each day. Every dawn brought a new and more spectacular panorama, and with it a bit more of despair's weight fell from my shoulders.

We stayed far from the places of men, voyaging into rugged territories with only one another for companionship. Chyrizah and I came to depend upon one another, and in turn support one another.

As our journey progressed, I came to realize that even if our venture ended in failure, if we perished before ever reaching the Sanctuary Isle, I would not have traded the experience. I had been witness to unforgettable beauty. I had known the sweet taste of freedom.

And I had known love.

More than once we were reminded of the fate from which we had escaped, a fate that so many others still shared. Worse, it was not within our power to help those who were still shackled by the chains of slavery. We could only cling to the shadows and watch the misery of others.

The capture, either dead or alive, of escaped slaves is a lucrative business. More than once we managed to avoid being taken by one hunter or another, though we owed our escapes – some far more narrow than I care to remember – as much to luck as to our own ingenuity.

I had heard tales of a Lesser Races bounty hunter who preyed upon his own kind, but I dismissed the notion. I could not bring myself to believe such a thing was possible.

The instances of danger we endured were outnumbered by those of utter peace. Avalon's panorama spread itself before us, a splendor I came to think of as an expansive reflection of the freedom we had claimed for ourselves.

We traversed the spine of the world, moving ever westward toward the coast and the Great Sea beyond.

At times I would think of those who had wrested the Tournament Isle from the kingdoms of the East and West. Two humans of royal blood, a Heron prince and a Raven princess, had turned their backs upon their lineage in order give the Lesser Races a place of freedom. True freedom, not the servitude and repression – if not actual slavery – to which our brethren in Heron lands are subjected.

Though I could not fathom why humans would choose to aid our people, I could understand the courage demanded by such an act of defiance. It is the same courage of a slave defying a master.

Many of the threats that had dogged our trail fell away as we climbed higher into the mountains. The snow-choked passes, however, held dangers all their own.

after F.F.

But we were not those same fearful slaves who had slunk through a broken fence and into the covering darkness. We had learned to overcome the hardships in our path, and grasped life with the tenacity of those who understand how fleeting it can be. We fought for our survival.

We killed for it.

I've no idea how many days had passed before we smelled the tang of salt in the air. Though I know it could have been no more than a few hours, it seemed an eternity before we crested a bluff and finally beheld the Great Sea. So much water, more than could ever possibly exist to the eyes of one who had never seen so much as a tarn. Its sheer, unbroken immensity, reaching as far as the eye could see and beyond, generated equal parts exhilaration and foreboding within me.

We built a boat from what could be scavenged, sometimes taking from the beach, other times traveling leagues for some necessary binding or scrap.

M y hands knew the tilling of soil, not the raising of sails or tacking against the wind. How could I, whose earliest memories are of working the earth, ever hope to be a sailor? And yet, I had been born a slave, and found the strength to be something else.

Even before we escaped the estate we had taught ourselves to locate a direction by reading the stars in the night sky. It's what allowed us to stay our course west across the land. Continuing across the sea would be no different.

I was enough of a realist to know we stood a far better chance of drowning, or perishing from exposure, than we did of ever reaching our goal. But we had not come so far and sacrificed so much to stop short. We set sail and placed ourselves in the hands of providence as fair winds pushed us into the unknown. The entirety of our journey, of our attempt at grasping freedom, had been a voyage into the unknown.

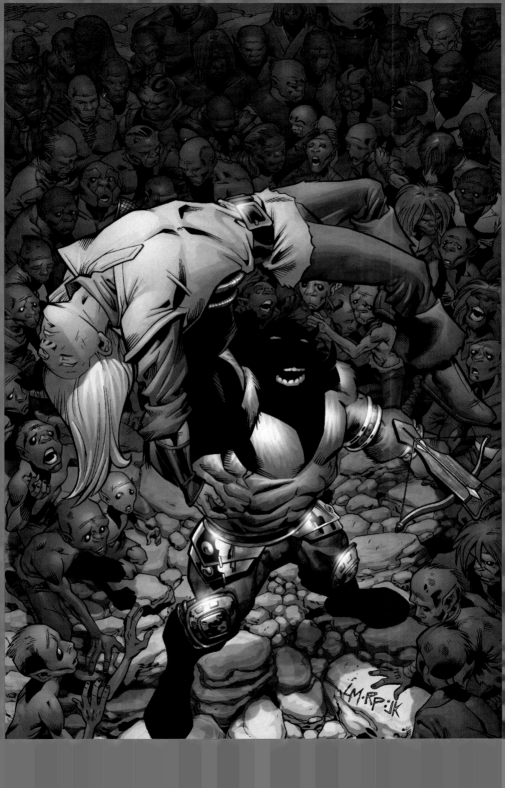

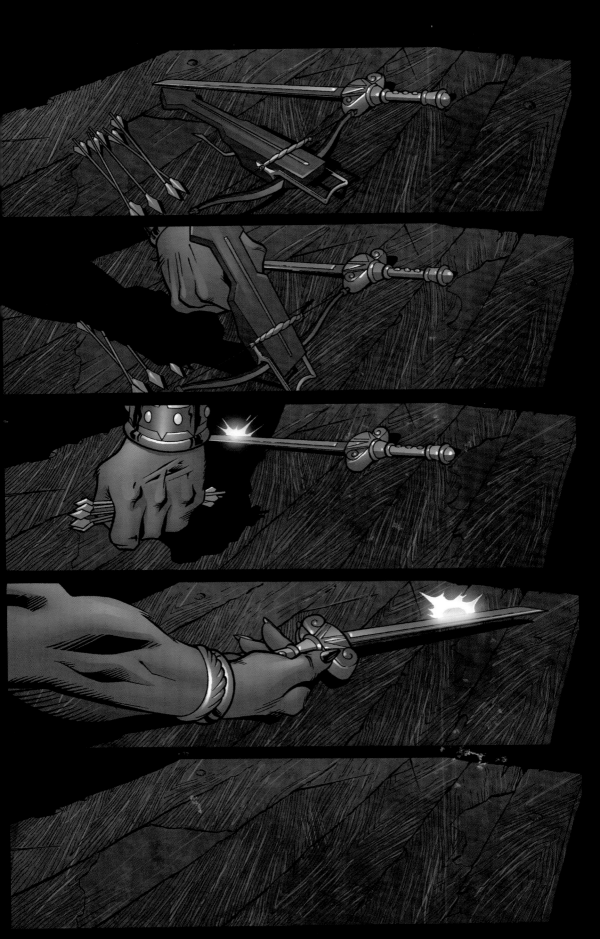

HE'S HIS OWN MAN NOW, KAI. HE'S A FAR CRY FROM THE BOY WE SENT OFF TO THE TOURNAMENT ON HIS TWENTY-FIRST BIRTHDAY.

HIS *OWN* MAN?

HE DIDN'T SEEM TO HAVE ANY QUALMS ABOUT TAKING UP RESIDENCE IN THE HERON COMPOUND.

ETHAN!

ETHAN, *OPEN UP!* IT'S TIME WE...

WHUMP

...WE...

GOOD MORNING, KAI...

WE'LL BE LEAVING OON. I CAME TO SAY GOODBYE.

AND TO *TALK*.

SIT WITH ME.

OF COURSE.

ETHAN, I KNOW YOU'RE *SURE* ABOUT WHAT YOU'RE DOING AND I WOULDN'T BEGIN TRYING TO TALK YOU OUT OF IT.

I'VE KNOWN WHICH OF MY SONS WAS THE *HEADSTRONG* ONE SINCE YOU WERE OLD ENOUGH TO WALK.

I UNDERSTAND YOU'RE COMMITTED TO WHAT YOU'VE BEGUN HERE, AND TO MAKING THIS ISLAND YOUR HOME.

I AM.

YOU'VE ACCOMPLISHED A GREAT DEAL. ALMOST THE IMPOSSIBLE.

AND I'M *PROUD* OF YOU.

A FREE NATION FOR THE LESSER RACES WILL DRASTICALLY CHANGE THE FACE OF THE RAVEN KINGDOM AS WELL AS OUR OWN.

I SUPPOSE I SHOULD HAVE *EXPECTED* THIS, CONSIDERING THE CLOSENESS OF YOUR RELATIONSHIP WITH SKINK SINCE YOU WERE A CHILD.

SOMETIMES I THINK *HE* WAS AS MUCH A PARENT TO YOU AS YOUR MOTHER AND I WERE.

IN OUR LANDS THE LESSER RACES ENJOY THE SEMBLANCE OF FREEDOM *SERVITUDE* BESTOWS UPON THEM.

BUT I SUSPECT A GREAT MANY WILL YIELD TO THE LURE THIS SANCTUARY ISLAND REPRESENTS.

THE HERON KINGDOM WILL HAVE TO COME TO TERMS WITH THAT.

AND *YOU* WILL HAVE A GREAT DEAL TO COME TO TERMS WITH AS WELL.

UNDERSTAND WHAT YOU'RE ABOUT TO EMBARK UPON, ETHAN. IF I CAN TEACH YOU ANYTHING...

...IT'S THAT LEADERSHIP IS FAR MORE *BURDEN* THAN *BLESSING*.

YOU ARE THEIR *SAVIOR* NOW, MY SON. BUT YOU ARE NOT *ONE* OF THEM.

WHAT WILL YOU BE TO THEM IN A *MONTH*, OR A *YEAR*, SAVE A REMINDER OF THEIR FORMER MASTERS?

ONCE THIS EUPHORIA OF FREEDOM PASSES, YOU WILL ALL BE LEFT WITH THE REALITY OF HOW YOU WILL LIVE YOUR LIVES HERE.

HOW DO YOU EVEN KNOW THEY WILL *ACCEPT* YOU?

I NEVER THOUGHT IT WOULD BE *EASY*.

IT WON'T BE. YOU'VE LED THEM TO THEIR PROMISED LAND...

...BUT THIS ISLAND WASN'T BUILT TO BE INHABITED YEAR ROUND. IT WAS BUILT TO B POPULATED BUT A FORTNIGHT A YEA

HOW WILL YOU FEED THEM, CLOTHE THEM, SHELTER THEM?

THESE ARE CIRCUMSTANCES I HAVE NEVER FACED, AND I AM NOT SO PRESUMPTUOUS TO BELIEVE I KNOW HOW TO ADVISE YOU...

...BUT I WILL TELL YOU *THIS*.

YOU ARE MY SON, AND IF THERE IS A WAY TO MAKE THIS DREAM WORK, I KNOW *YOU* WILL FIND IT.

I LOVE YOU MORE THAN LIFE ITSELF ETHAN. I LOVE YOU ENOUGH TO *LET YOU GO*.

THANK YOU, FATHER.

I LOVE YOU, TOO.

THE GIRL? ASHLEIGH?

SHE'S THAT IMPORTANT TO YOU?

MORE THAN I CAN SAY.

SHE OPENED MY EYES TO SO MUCH. I CAN HARDLY BELIEVE SHE AND BRON SPRANG FROM THE SAME SIRE.

IT *WEIGHS* ON ME, NOT KNOWING FOR CERTAIN IF BRON PERISHED.

NOT KNOWING IF I WAS ABLE TO AVENGE ARTOR.

YOUR MOTHER IS MORE CONCERNED WITH *YOU* THAN YOUR *VOW*. SHE IS RELIEVED, BUT *ANXIOUS* TO SEE YOU.

I WANT YOU TO *VISIT* AS SOON AS YOU ARE ABLE.

I WILL.

FATHER, WHAT ABOUT KAI AND YLENA? WITH EVERYTHING THAT'S HAPPENED...

HERE HE COMES!

YOU HAVE BEEN SO VERY PATIENT, AND I THANK YOU FOR THAT.

I KNOW YOU'VE BEEN WAITING FOR ANSWERS, AND I WISH...

...*I WISH* I COULD TELL YOU I KNEW WHAT THOSE ANSWERS ARE.

...YOU'VE RISKED *EVERYTHING* TO JOURNEY HERE IN HOPES OF BUILDING A NEW LIFE...

...A BETTER LIFE THAN THE ONE OFFERED BY THE SHACKLES YOU LEFT BEHIND.

YOUR COURAGE IS *EXTRAORDINARY*.

WE'VE ACCOMPLISHED SO MUCH ALREADY. WE'VE CARVED A NEW HOME FOR OURSELVES.

BUT WE'VE MADE ONLY THE *FIRST STEP* ON THIS JOURNEY.

...EXETER, *NO!*

THIS *ISN'T* GOING TO BE OUR WAY.

HE TRIED TO *KILL* YOU, ETHAN. YOU CAN'T ACTUALLY ALLOW HIM TO SURVIVE.

IDEALISM IS A PLEASANT CONCEIT, BUT YOU MUST BE PRAGMATIC IF YOU EVER INTEND TO BE—

NO.

I WILL NOT HAVE THIS KINGDOM FOUNDED UPON AN *EXECUTION.* TAKE HIM TO THE SHORE, PUT HIM IN A BOAT, *EXILE* HIM.

BUT I *WON'T* HAVE HIM KILLED. DO YOU UNDERSTAND ME?

I UNDERSTAND YOU BETTER THAN YOU KNOW, ETHAN.

I *SPIT* ON YOUR FALSE MERCY, *HUMAN!*

YOU LACK EVEN THE COURAGE TO *SLAY ME!*

ENOUGH.

NH

I'LL SEND HIM ON HIS WAY.

AND I'LL...

NF

...DO WHAT I HAVE TO DO.

YOU *HEARD* HIM, DIDN'T YOU? HE SAID YOU DIDN'T THROW OFF YOUR CHAINS SO YOU COULD CALL ME MASTER.

I KNOW THAT...

...BUT DO *YOU?*

DO YOU THINK OF ME AS AN OUTSIDER? DO YOU SEE ME *DIFFERENTLY* THAN YOU SEE YOURSELVES?

THOSE ARE THE *OLD* WAYS, AND THEY HAVE NO PLACE HERE. WE MUST NO LONGER THINK OF HUMANS AND LESSER RACES SEPARATELY, ROYAL BORN OR SLAVE BORN.

HERE WE MUST BE *ONE* IF WE ARE TO SURVIVE. *THAT'S* THE ONLY ANSWER I HAVE FOR YOU.

EVERYTHING ELSE WE'LL DECIDE AS WE GO. IT'S YOURS TO DECIDE IF YOU WANT ME TO *LEAD* YOU.

OR IF YOU EVEN WANT ME TO *STAY* HERE.

ETHAN!

ETHAN!

ETHAN!

ETHAN!

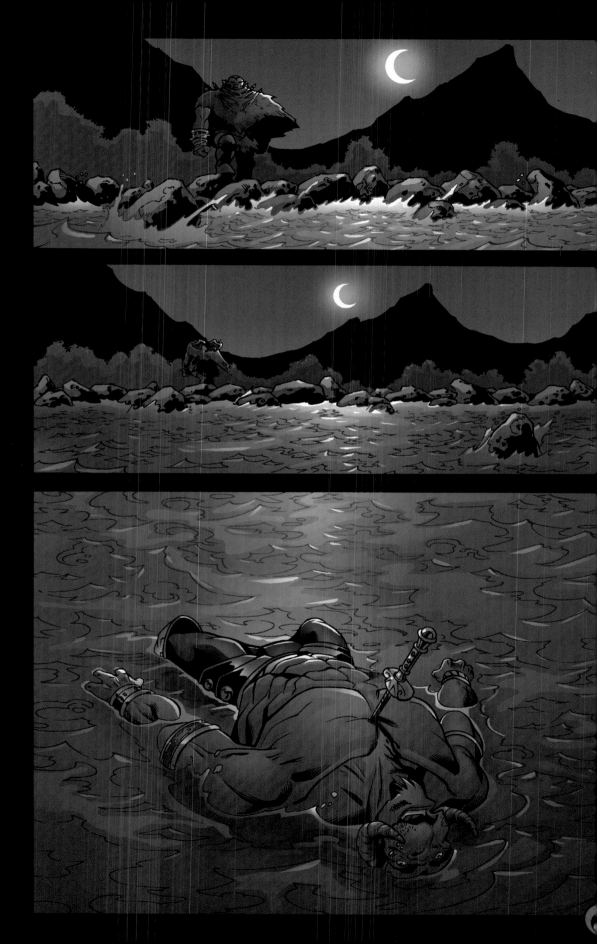

"With SCION the job was making everything believable, even though it was all created from scratch."
— Jim Cheung

THE WORLD ——— ACCORDING TO ——— CHEUNG

Jim Cheung is the only one of CrossGen's original quartet of pencilers still drawing the same title. More than three years later, he has stamped SCION as his own creation, a carefully researched and constructed world that seems undeniably real despite its fantastic setting.

"I used as much historical reference as I could get. Even though this is a fantasy world, it's all based around the medieval period. The high-tech aspect comes from a mix of *Star Wars* and the latest sci-fi DVDs I can get my hands on."

His protracted stay on the book has allowed him to bring a depth to the world of Avalon and its inhabitants not often seen in monthly comics.

"I've been on SCION longer than anyone in the studio has been on any project, longer than my stint on *X-Force* for Marvel. It's been good because I've been able to build upon it and develop deeper layers. When you first start on a project like this, it's brand new, there's no history to draw upon. A lot of the elements are very basic to begin with, and over time you discover what works and what doesn't and refine both the visuals and your technique."

Jim shared his thoughts on a few of the pieces contained in this volume:

"One of my favorite characters to draw is Exeter. It's always fun to draw the big dudes. I wanted this particular shot to reflect his menace, and the cast shadows help convey that."

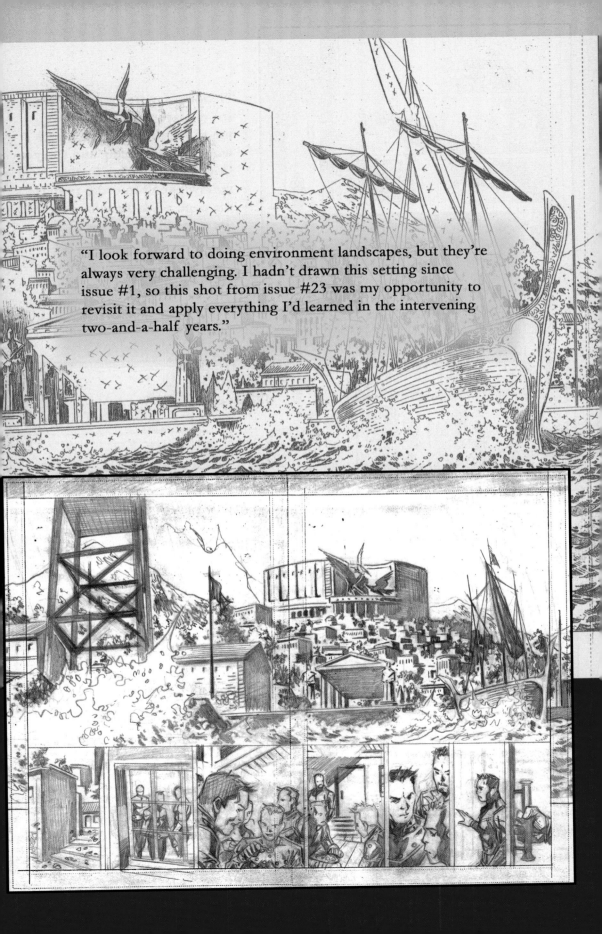

"I look forward to doing environment landscapes, but they're always very challenging. I hadn't drawn this setting since issue #1, so this shot from issue #23 was my opportunity to revisit it and apply everything I'd learned in the intervening two-and-a-half years."

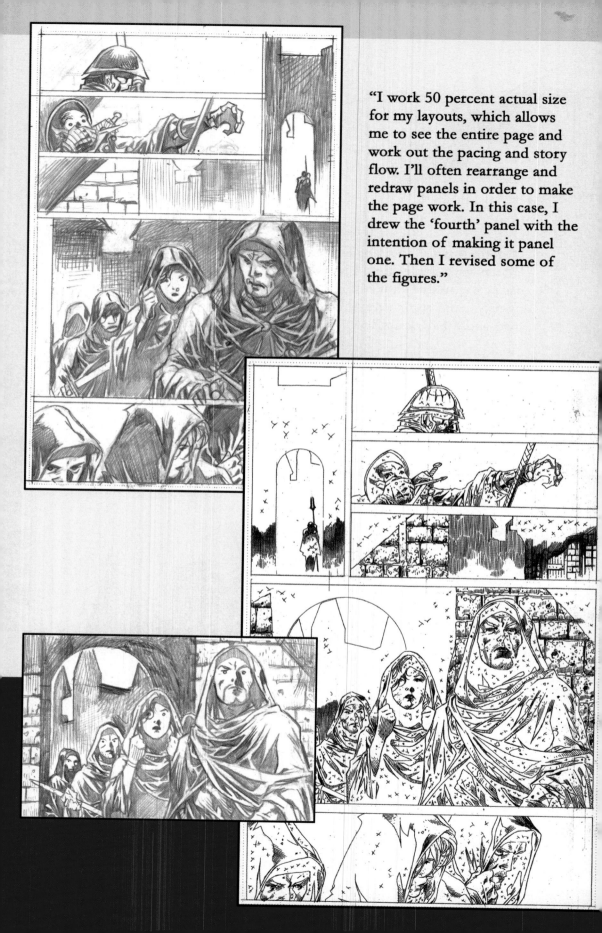

"I work 50 percent actual size for my layouts, which allows me to see the entire page and work out the pacing and story flow. I'll often rearrange and redraw panels in order to make the page work. In this case, I drew the 'fourth' panel with the intention of making it panel one. Then I revised some of the figures."

"I had a fairly strong idea in my head of what I wanted for the final image of the cover. It's a favorite because it was the result of a collaborative effort amongst the entire team. The ghosting effect with Ethan was Justin Ponsor's idea, and really helped enhance the impression of the energy being unleashed. Kudos to Justin for helping me pull it off."

CROSSGEN COMICS®
GRAPHIC NOVELS